I0610922

# ONCE UPON A *Time* THERE WERE TWO SOUL MATES

Don Ryan

ISBN    978-1-64552-023-8    (Paperback)
ISBN    978-1-64552-024-5    (Digital)

Lettra Press books may be ordered through booksellers or by contacting:

Lettra Press LLC
18229 E 52nd Ave.
Denver City, CO 80249
1 303 586 1431 | info@lettrapress.com
www.lettrapress.com

# Contents

# Prologue

This is an incredible story of a couple born on the same day, in the same hospital one hour apart.

This story would have not happened, unless the author had waited to the last minute to ask Nancy to go with him to the "Senior Prom". After the "Prom Acceptance", this story erupts with none stop action. The story is part fiction, except for the true experiences we both had. The flying jobs, educational degrees, military, and the places they had been. The rest was filled in to make the experiences complete.

The Author uses this knowledge as a senior adult for young people to not to lose heart, and ask God for all things, if you want this to become reality. Therefore, don't set there like a wall flower, but hang on, the "Curtains of your life experience is about to part and the you and your intended one will be on Stage"! Just like happened to the couple, in "Once a Upon a Time, There Were Two Soul Mates"! It can happen to you.

# The Prom Proposal

It was the last week of January on a Friday morning, 1952 prior to lunch, as we were setting down for our physics class. Don came out of "No Where", and gave Nancy a card with her name beautifully crafted on it. And inside the envelope was a request to meet Don for lunch after class, in scripted letters. After class they met and, with the smile Don love so much, "The shadow of her smile", Nancy accepted the invitation. As they were going down the stairs, Don Said, "Nancy find a quiet place where we can eat and talk". I will buy, and I will bring the trays. We had our lunch with small talk. Don said, "Nancy we have about 4 months to go before graduation, what are you going to do the rest of your life?" Don I wanted to go Kent State University and become Primary grade school teacher, but my parent could not afford to send me. Things are really tough financially. Dad suggested he could help get me a job at the Goodyear Tire and Rubber Company, in order for me to pay my own way. By this time we were running out of time until the next class. Don said, "Nancy have you made a commitment for the Senior Prom yet?" She said, "No". Would you like to go with me, and Nancy said, without hesitation "Yes, I would". Nancy can I take you home after class in my old 1941 Pontiac? Nancy said, "Yes".

I would like to get your mother's approval to have breakfast with you in the morning, if you approve, Nancy said, "certainly", besides it is Saturday.

I, also, wanted to spend the day with, you to show you how I make my living.

You will not be bored! (Little did Nancy know what was coming?)

Don took Nancy home, and introduces him to Mrs. Kelly. Mrs. Kelly was impressed with Don's stature and into mature young man that he had become.

He, also, express desire to keep Nancy until 5 P.M.

He wanted to show Nancy how he made his living. Mrs. Kelley approved.

Don said," Nancy see you at 7:30 AM tomorrow".

Don bid everyone a good day and returned to his home. Mrs. Kelly Said,"

Nancy, what was that all about"! Mom, it looks like my first date will be a breakfast date. He it will be interesting to see what he does.

He told me it would not be boring,

Nancy had a good relationship with her Mom. Mrs. Kelley had a heart to heart talk with Nancy. Nancy was the last of 3 girls in the family. And Mrs. Kelly was quite protective of her. Their only son was 12 yrs. old and not a problem yet. Nancy describes the whole affair.

Don came up to her at the beginning of Physics class out of "Out of nowhere", and said," I believe this note is for you Nancy. Mom it was beautifully done with Washington lithogram on the back label watermark with "Nancy" written in cryptography on the on the label. Don had to go to his seat because the bell had rung. I opened the note and it said, "Will you have lunch with me after class?" Mom do you want to see it? Mrs. Kelley looked at the invitation and noted then only one similar she had seen was in Washington D.C. during a trip there. Little did

Nancy know it will play a part of her future? Don became scarce around Springfield H.S. after his freshman year. After lettering in most sports, also, he was straight "A" student in the top of the class. Now that I think of it, Don always kind of looked after me. I really never thought I had a chance with him. He was always seem to be busy. I never saw him dating other girls. I once had a problem with math, he was a good teacher, and help bring my grade from a "D" to an "A". That why when he ask me to the Senior Prom it was such a surprise, "I am still in shock". Look Mom before he left he gave me his athletic sweater to wear at school this is a coveted prize all girls like to would get. To be frank, I did not think anybody would ask me, especially Don.

Nancy it been my experience that a dates out of nowhere are the most dangerous. I would not miss the next episode of this story in a heartbeat!

# The Breakfast Invitation

I picked up Nancy for breakfast at 7:30AM. Instead of going to some local restaurant I headed for the Akron Munipcal Airport. When we pulled in, this caused a look of puzzlement to Nancy, but she did not say anything. She had a 2/3 length white leather-like coat, black slacks, scarf, a white turtle neck sweater, and brown penny loafers. When arriving at Akron Airport, I was wearing Southern Air's uniform of tan slacks, (black shiny shoes. Shorty demanded this), brown airline shirt, black tie, with our companies wings on the left pocket. My name was stenciled underneath: Capt. Don Ryan.

On the right pocket was stenciled Southern Air Cargo Airline and Mail.

Also, on the shoulders were the epilates with four bars of the Captains Rating. All of this was covered up with a smart brown leather jacket, so that Nancy could not see it, but she will at breakfast in Cleveland. We walked to the desk of Southern Cargo Airlines that was staffed by a middle aged woman by the name of "Hazel". Hazel ran operations, more too, you always wanted to be on the good side of Hazel.

Hazel said," Where is Bob"? It is your day off. I said," I was doing his Cleveland pick up and bringing it back to Akron". He needed the morning off so that he could take his wife for a medical check up. They are expecting their first child. His wife is 3 months pregnant. Bob will finish the trip to Pittsburg and Washington, D.C. Now, hearing all of this, Nancy found we were going to Cleveland, and while there will have breakfast. We will going to Burke Lakefront Airport.

Hazel said," What restaurant"? I said, "The Barge Restaurant, at the end of Runway 9". Hazel said, "An excellent choice".

Are going to take this nice young lady with you? "Yes", I said. As Nancy left the building going to the aircraft ramp, Nancy said, "Don you have to be kidding"! I said, "I am starving, plus I have to get the mail to Cleveland". As we were coming up to the planes, she said, "I have not been this close to an airplane this big". I told her that the planes with the Southern Cargo Airlines/Mail carry mainly mail in a "Star Route Contract with the Postal Service". Much of the mail is high security mail on a route from Cleveland, Pittsburg, Washington, D.C. and Columbus, Ohio.

I told Nancy we could carry up to 2500 pounds of mail or cargo. The speed of the ship is 211 mph. top altitude is 22,500 ft., and range with the long range tanks is 1000 miles. We have 3 airplanes, all are twin beeches 18's with two super charged 450 hp Pratt and Whitney engines. Nancy asked, "How many people will it hold". I told her five passengers and one or two pilots. We did the prefight together. I felt the more she knew the less anxious she would become in the flying part. We had a flight plan on file, which is standard procedure with airlines and government contractors . Nancy said, "How long have You been doing all this"? I said, "At this level, one and one half Years". While you guys were enjoying your summer vacations, I was in aviation school learning aerodynamics, engines, airframes, etc.

I hold a multiengine, commercial, and instrument rating, along with type rating in the Twin B-18 (C-45). I am the youngest pilot on the line. Let's mount up and get the show on the road. We got into the plane, and the first thing she said, "This really looks complicated".

I said is not if you know where everything is and how to use it.

If, I told my friends back a school, no one will believe me!

I said," Tell no one, it is our secret"!

I got her into the copilot's seat and strapped her in.

I gave her the standard safety briefing, evacuation of the aircraft, use of oxygen mask of the bulkhead behind her seat in case we had to go above 10,000ft., talking on the radio etiquette ( a small button on the intercom part the control column, if she wanted to talk to me), and when not to talk to me. At this point on the companies frequency I alerted Carl, our mechanic to prop the engines and to ready to pull the chocks out from the wheels, I started the left engine (the side all the generators where on). Then the right engine. I bad to run the engines at 1000 rpm to get temperature range in order to check the props and fuel mixture settings. It also gave me time to set up my radio frequencies for communications. I listened for the ATIS for weather and Airport Conditions.

After receiving all of that information, on the company radio I asked Carl to pull the chocks from the wheels. I contacted Akron Area Control Tower on frequency 134.75 that twin Beech 243 was ready to taxi to the active runway. Akron Tower said, "Approved to taxi to Runway 28 and hold".

I requested a right turn out (towards Cleveland), The control tower operator said", Altimeter 30.18, Beech 243 is cleared to 3000 ft. direct, to Burke Lakefront Airport, contact Cleveland Center on 135.00 after leaving the pattern". You are cleared for take-off and have a good trip. Beech 243, Thank you! At this time the tail wheel was locked and full power applied to the throttles and lift off established.

THE CLEVELAND BREAKFAST TRIP WAS ON!

# Cleveland Breakfast

Cleveland Center cleared our airplane to Pattern Altitude at Burke Lakeside Airport. We then we left Cleveland Center and contacted Burke Tower on frequency 124.3 to let them know we are coming.

Burke Tower instructed us to do an overhead of the airport and join runway 06 on the downwind leg at 1000 ft. I had already switched on my landing light, which was noticed by Nancy. I explained to her that the FAA (Federal Aviation Administration) requires this of all aircraft within 10 nautical miles of an airport to help in traffic separation. So coming off downwind on 06 and joining the approach to 06, we were cleared by the tower to land. At the outer marker, approach speed was attained and the flaps were lower to (slows and increased the angle of attack of the airplane), cowl flaps on the engines full (full to cool the engines at high power and low airspeed), full props, gear down (2 green lights), plus other less critical items on the check list. We are now lined up for landing on Runway 06. The landing was a "grease on", a term use by pilots for a perfect landing, which I needed that day. For I heard distinct sighing of relief from the right seat passenger.

After we landed the tower gave me ground control on frequency 124.3. I asked directions to the U.S. Mail drop, and they directed me to taxiway to the U.S. Mail Facilities. I parked and shut down. Mail personnel came to unload the reload the mail. We were in a highly restricted area and I had to get a pass for Nancy to wear. I laughed and told her, she was a marked woman. In fact they told me I was responsible for her. I showed Nancy to the women's room and she did not refuse. I ask the manager if I could use one of his golf carts to go to the restaurant. He said," Being a contractor for us I don't see why not". I said, "My flight plan has me leaving in 2 hours", and I will be back in an hour and 14. We will be at the "Barge Restaurant". He knew my return route Akron direct Pittsburg direct Washington, D.C..

Just then Nancy came out of the women's bathroom, proudly displaying Her temporary identication badge, I already had a permanent one on a Lanyard. Now we boarded the golf cart for the "Barge Restaurant'.

As we sat down for breakfast, I removed my jacket, she looked shocked to see the rest of my uniform ,which made all of what I had said real to her, I asked Nancy," How was the trip"? She said, "It left me breathless"!

I even forgot to talk to you on the radio. I said," We will take care of that on the way back".

We had a super breakfast that morning. It really was the beginning of our binding together. I fold her now you know the other side of me. My pursuit of other interests, left me no time for dates and other school activities. Professional Aviation that I am pursuing matures one quickly. You pass muster or you don't survive. You have to stay current flying, or the next FAA check ride could be your last. Plus, you must stay physically fit. High School is really mundane. I have been so busy that certain aspects of my life were over looked! I thought about you on flight back from Washington, the Thursday prior to Friday when I asked you to the prom. I thought, this is the girl I secretly loved and I may have lost an opportunity of the lifetime due my negligence. Well Don that answered the question where you got the beautiful card you gave me. Yes, Nancy I had it made at Washington Airport.

When, I asked you to the Prom, and you said, "Yes", it was in the nick of time. After all we have been together since birth, let's make it always. We are not done with today, by the end of this day your world will be turn upside down.

After a great breakfast. We prepare to return to Akron with the new mail, that was destined to Washington through Pittsburg. Nancy said, "Do you ever fly this plane to Washington, D.C."? "Yes, I said", every Saturday and some Sundays. Nancy Said," What other destination's do you go"? As a Star Route Contractor, we, also, go to Columbus, Cincinnati, and Toledo.

We took the golf car back and thanked the manager for its use. When Nancy was in the bathroom, I supervised the loading of the cargo of mail. We had a cargo net on each side of the cargo hold that would hold 2500 lbs. of mail each. I had to make sure all the mail was accurately weighed for the weight and balance calculations', and to make sure the cargo was tied down properly. I signed the final documents, and we were good to go!

On our fight plan back to Akron, had the same numbers in reverse. Burke Tower cleared us for takeoff and we were on our way. On our trip to Akron Nancy learned how to use the intercom , and I had a "virtual chatter box in the right seat". From a quiet little girl as I knew her to a young lady excited about flying.

We had an uneventful trip back to Akron. I met "Bob" and I introduce him to Nancy. Now she was officially part of the gang. He thanked me for helping him out. 1 asked, "how is you wife"? He excitedly said, "They were expecting a boy in 7 months."

I told Bob not to expect any weather all the way to Washington, D.C.

I did the final paperwork for "Hazel" and gave it to her. She ask Nancy "How was the breakfast"? Nancy said it was the best breakfast she has ever had! This brought a long stare my way from "Hazel".

Hazel thanked me for helping Bob out on my day off. Hazel didn't know how she help me out. In fact she talked quietly to Nancy not thinking I could hear her. Hazel said," to Nancy, You should latch on to Capt. Don, he is a nice guy, and one of our finest pilots", I was in shock to pick up on the conversation between the two. It was a sure bet Hazel had approved of Nancy. I thought, what a match maker Hazel was and behind my back at that! At that we turned to leave, where upon Hazel winked at me, knowing full well I have heard everything. We went out to our "Old 1941 Pontiac". I told Nancy we had to check on a car. Again, I got that questionable look from Nancy. It was time for my car to change

# "The Car, Dinner, and Beyond"

So as Nancy and Don where leaving in the Pontiac, I informed her is about 1:30 PM and I had to check on a car at Schooner Chevalier, in Hartville, about 10 miles from Akron and 3-4 miles from the large newly constructed airport called the Akron-Canton Airport. After the car, I had to stop by to check the progress on the status of the new hanger being constructed for Southern Cargo Air Ways/Mail. It was going to be big enough to hold the twin beech's and the two new DC-3'S which we due to be delivered at end of June. I had to make sure, with the contractor that the ramp and hanger would hold all the aircraft. Also, I need to know when we can move in. We had to have a maintenance area, and office space for Hazel, her staff, our offices, cargo holding area, and an area for rest relaxation and refreshments. When all airplanes are operational, we expect to have 10 regular pilots, with three in reserve. Carl will pick up 8 mechanics to keep them ail flying. Hazel will have 8 new office personnel and 3 part time floats. Hazel has asked, specifically you to be one her part time floats. We went to Akron Canton for expansion and the new ILS landing system in bad weather, and longer runways I know that you have a lot of questions, but they will have to wait after dinner, and a couple of other things much more important! We will get to those things in detail later. It was 2:00 PM when they pulled into the dealership. I checked with the Manager, and he said," the pickup was tricked out with everything I ordered". The company radio had been installed with antennas to communicate with our office as well with ATC. It had sheepskin seat covers to cover the bench seats, suburban all weather tires, radio, heater, automatic gearing, a riding and comfort and quiet kit. It was dark green, with a gold strip around the cab. It also, had a mahogany lining in the truck bed. In short it was a real honey! I had already budgeted and paid for it in cash. (In 1953 this truck sold for $1300 dollars) They brought the finished truck out and I gave the manager my old faithful 1941 Pontiac keys. He gave me the new keys, and a set for Nancy. She said, "What a beautiful truck".

What are these keys for? I told her, they are your set; you will need them in the future, again I got this little smile! We got in and it started like a dream, and we were off to see the new hanger and then dinner at the 356th Fighter Squadron restaurant on the Southside of Airport.

**1953 Chevrolet 3100 5 window Pickup Truck**

# Dinner Of a lifetime

Upon arriving at the new hanger construction site, we checked it out so we could report back to "Shorty? Smith. The foreman of the project Said, "You can plan on moving in March, 1952, really one month earlier than we expected". I was sure that "Shorty" would be pleased at the news. So it was off to dinner at the 356th, a rather upscale restaurant. I had pre-emptively, earlier in the week, reserved a table with the manager of the restaurant for a good view if the airport and private. I had 2 and one haft hours to make my next proposal to "Nancy". It would turn out to be the most important decisions of our young lives! Nancy was delighted with the table and the ambiance of it. She said, "Don I have never been in a place as nice as this before". We had a sumptuous dinner. As we were talking small talk, I asked, "Nancy I have a very important question", and I said", a lot depends upon your answer". Nancy said, "What is the question"?

With all the courage I could muster, I asked Nancy," Would you marry me"?

Nancy lovingly looked into my eyes with shadow of her smile and said, "Yes".

I said, "Let seal it with a kiss.

Once my heart stop pounding, I found out later, Nancy had the same reaction. From this on in all things we do is together, especially for the future. Did these 24 hours turn your world upside down? I said it would, and we have just begun! I have some good concrete plans for the future. Let me talk to your Dad and Mom for your hand in marriage, before you talk to them. I believe this is the proper way to go. I think it would be wise to do this toward the end of February. This would allow your family get used to me and you to me together. Also, it will give more time for Planning. Don took Nancy Home after dinner. It was 5:00 P.M., which was the time he promised Mrs. Kelly he would bring Nancy home. On the way home Nancy became rather quiet. Don mentioned this to her. And Nancy said, "What did you expect Don!" I started out this day on what I thought was a Breakfast date with you! In turn you flew me on my first plane ride to Cleveland for breakfast, and I thought I was going to die, then I accepted your marriage proposal, found out in my wildest dreams, I was going to Kent State for college and living there as your wife, and "Oh" yes, I accepted your prom proposal, that started this change of events. I just thinking, I am to wake up from this dream, and if do I will be really disappointed. And, Don you wonder why I have become quiet. I am trying to sort all of this out in my head.

As they arrived at Nancy's House they were several cars in the driveway. Nancy said, "Her Mom made would make a spaghetti dinner on some Saturday nights for the family". With a "twitter" Nancy said, Mom designed it to let everyone check you out Don. Mrs. Kelly had Don and Nancy come in and introduce Don. Mrs. Kelley said to Don to take off his jacket and have some coffee. Nancy had told Mrs. Kelly they had eaten. Also. Nancy brought in two wrapped pictures for her wall.

When Mrs. Kelly took Don's jacket, she noticed the rest of his uniform, as did the rest of the family. Mr. Kelly with large cigar told Nancy, who did you bring home this time? Mrs, Kelly admonish him for his rudeness and Don looked Mr. Kelly in the eye with a look he never will forget. So the evening did not start well. Mr. Kelly pressed on. Nancy, I want a full accounting with this guy! Don said," Mr. Kelly the name you are searching for is "Capt. Don Ryan". Nervously, Nancy began her explanation with the prom proposal & the 7:30 AM breakfast date. Mr. Kelly "said, a breakfast date? " Yes, Dad he took me to Akron Airport, to Southern Airlines/mail, where he is a pilot and flew me and the mail to Cleveland, Mr. Kelly said," what in a "Piper Cub"?

No Dad, Don gave me pictures of the plane we flew in. Here, I will get them for you. When she showed her Dad, one of Nancy's brother-in-law's said, to Mr. Kelly, "That is like a small airliner"!

At that point then ashes fell off of Mr, Kelly in to his coffee. Mrs. Kelly stifled a muffled laugh! Nancy pressed on, that Don carried high security mail between Cleveland, Akron, Pittsburg, and Washington D.C..Nancy when on Detailing the entire flight from Akron to Cleveland. Altitudes, radio transmissions, and landing at Cleveland. We had fabulous breakfast there at Barge's restaurant. It is part of a maritime display of the great lakes. This was the Breakfast part of the date. I had to get a temporary pass to enter the high security area. Here it is on this lanyard around my neck. We borrow a post office golf cart to go to the restaurant. The postal employees loaded on the mail cargo. Don had to do something called weight and balance & sign some papers. Don did the preflight, filed the flight plan, we strapped in and were cleared for take-off. We came back to Akron at 8,000ft. Upon landing Don pointed out Springfield Lake, our house, and then the runway.

We landed, I got to meet the Southern Airways/mail crew. The mail we delivered will be going to Washington, D.C. via Bob another pilot.

# 1953 Chevrolet 3100 5 window Pickup Truck

We then headed for the Hartville Schooner's Chevalier Dealership. We pulled in and greeted by the manager. Don had ordered a beautiful pickup truck, Dark green with a gold stripe around the cab, mahogany bed trim, 4 wheel drive, hush kit, power steering, automatic transmission, suburban all weather tires, and installed is a VHP radio and antenna that he can talk to ATC (Tower) and Company radio). Dad we gave the manager the old 1941 Pontiac keys and left for our next assignment, to check progress on the construction of the new Southern Airways Hanger, at the Akron — Canton Airport. The construction manager said we will be ready transfer our 3 twin beeches and the 3 DC-3 in March. One of Nancy's brother-in-law ask what was DC-3. Nancy showed him one of the pictures. He exclaimed He saw an American Airlines plane at the airport that look just like that! Nancy said," Don been training to be a captain on the DC-3 and they will be operational in June, for Southern Airlines/Mail. Then we went to the

356th Squadron restaurant for supper. When finished we came here at 5:00PM as promised to Mom. So Dad here we are. You could have heard a pin drop at that point!

Nancy's Dad broke the silence when he asked Don where do plan to go next with my daughter? Mr. Kelly I would like to take her to church in the morning. The Springfield Fellowship Church, with Pastor Homer Burkett. It in the corner of Old Home Road & Ewart Road with your approval. Mr. Kelly said, "Yes, Yes, she can go!

With that Don again, said he was glad to have met the family, excused himself & bid everyone good night. He left Nancy's house with family setting stirring their coffee. After Nancy family departed, Nancy said, "Mom what a date we had today!" Her mother just rolled her eyes.

# "Future Plans"*

After the proposal for marriage was accepted, I felt the "Stage had been Set, and the Curtains Opened". The story of our future was about to begin. I will ask your parents for your hand in marriage. problem, the end of March we will become formally engaged. We could plan for the first or second week in June for a the Wedding and Reception. Also, your prom dress will be taken care of as well.

That is if you are in agreement with this plan.

We get your engagement /wedding ring in the first week of March.

I have a Saturday that week on my flight schedule for Washington.

I would like to take you with me to Washington on that day. We have three hour layover and that should be enough for lunch and business, We will go over the river to Alexandria, Va., to a place all Washingtonians get their jewelry called the "Diamond Mine".

I am sure you will be pleased with the selection. (Note: Don had made friends with "Gus" the gemologist who help make the selections in advance). The wedding rings set were in the range of $1000, and there was nothing in the Akron area that was even close to the quality of these gem's prices in todays market would be ten times a much .

After the selection we could have lunch while they were sizing the rings. Also, I want you and my sister Carol to get the ring size on my mother and your mother. I have ordered a diamond encrusted birthstone rings, your mother (blue) and my mother (green). After you put on your ring at engagement dinner then we will put their rings on. Of course I was sure they would choose the "Hartville Kitchen" for the occasion.

# "The Wedding Plans"

I would like you to wear a white wedding gown. I will have a tuxedo. We have been going to the Springfield Fellowship Church, is that O.K.? It is a small community church, pastured by the Rev. Homer Burkett.

I know both you and 1 feel comfortable there. If, you agree, let me know. Nancy said, "Yes, that would be great". Don't forget your folks as well as mine are not wealthy, but I can help with the wedding and reception costs. I will turn over to you, your selection of wedding announcements and other thing pertaining to the wedding, for I am out of my field on this one. Don't forget to include all Southern Air Crews on the guest list, and not but least please make Hazel a bridesmaids. After all, Hazel was responsible in part for all of this. Finally, after the wedding, I propose a Caribbean Cruise for a seven day trip out of Ft. Lauderdale, to unwind and get ready for our next adventure.

I have taken the liberty to reserve a nice set of rooms in the married section of the twin towers on the Kent State University Campus. I had to make the decision on this prior to our marriage plans, or I would have lost the reservation. It is a two bedroom two bath with a small kitchen and living room on the second floor with a great view overlooking the campus, and nearby woods and creek. It has a covered parking spot close to the back entrance. It will be an ideal lodging for our four years at KSU. The one bedroom we can turn into two offices, with book shelves, desks, and other accessories. Otherwise, the apartments are all fully furnished. I would suggest meal tickets for our suppers. The breakfasts and lunches we could do better in our apartment, due to our schedules. Just before our wedding we can get everything in order, groceries, school supplies, books, etc. So when we get back from our honeymoon, we will come from Cleveland to our apartment home, get ready for our summer session in college.

What do you think about these plans? Don, had never even thought that far ahead, with the thoughts of going to college or for that matter, or to marry you". These were things that dreams were made.

I didn't even think I had a chance of even going to the Prom until you asked me. I had no thoughts that you cared so much for me. I know I had, many of times thought about you, but though this was not a reality that would occur. It makes my head swim, I must be in some kind of a dream, but a good one!

I think you planning is great, and beyond my wildest dreams, but how are you going to afford all of this? I said," I thought you would never ask".

# A Summary of the Main Assets

Now that you have accepted my proposal for Marriage, I would like to discuss our net worth for us. All finances we can discuss between us. At this time my net worth is about $35,000. This is after I have budgeted all of our expenses to this point. The breakdown of investments was designed by Mr. Earl G, Smith, a Commercial realtor, stock broker, and developer of the First Central Bank Building in Akron. He had a summer place on Lake Erie, Mentor on the Lake. My mother was his domestic manager all things. I developed a close relationship with Mr. Smith and his three sons, who became U. S. Coast Guard Officers on Lake Erie Cutters. The treated me like I was one of their brothers. This is the reason I seemed to mature faster than kids of my age. They taught me to swim and sail on the lake. The financial plan Mr. Smith made for me was: One gold Krugerans per month, (Krugerans were going for $70, ($700 when I was 18 yrs. Old), 2 stocks, and Mr. Smith would advise me which ones such as IBM, financial institution etc.. At 14 yrs. old the stock market, DJ was just topping 500, and left over money I would put into CDs, and to keep $500 in the bank for emergencies. At 14 yrs. Old I was very busy: I had a 500 customer paper route, with 3 kids working for me. I gave them 100 papers a piece, and my self-200. 1 managed and did all the collections.

I really learned about people's behavior during that time, I made waterproof boxes to hold the papers. I made rounds with my old Cushman Motor Scooter carry the papers to the boxes and on my route. I sold my route to become a copy boy for the Akron Beacon Journal. When I was 15 yrs old. I gave this up later on, when I began to work for "Shorty". During the summer I worked for Motor's Inn, the trucking center across Rt. 224 were you lived. I would get the trucks at the Motor Inn restaurant and move them across the street, gas them up, check tires, and park them in a line on the ramp behind Motor's Inn. I had to have a special permit to do this job at 16. A "Yankee Line" instructor helped me to get my special commercial license. I had to take my truck drivers test in downtown Akron in traffic in a semi-trailer, which was no easy task. The state examiner, when 1 finished didn't say a thing, but wrote out my license and give it to me without fanfare. Along with this income, I augmented it with a trap line to catch muskrat and mink. We lived in a 25 square mile area of northern Ohio hardwoods with a good size creek transverse it. I found out some years back a flood at the headwaters of the creek destroyed a mink farm. The mink were wide spread down the creek, each pelt bringing $35-$40 dollars. I was harvesting 25-30 pelts a week, plus muskrats at $5 for a number one pelt.

I was harvesting 50 of these in addition. I kept this activity rather secret, to protect against poachers. They ruined my gold mine when the County dredged the creek. I am sure the mink reproduced like rats they were, so there was not a decreased in their population. They have probably found another spot to set up camp. I also, had a passion for flying. I belonged to the Rubber City Astronauts. We met at Hawk Field, a field just south of Tallmadge, an Akron Suburb. My event was the Tow Line Glider. Ours had a wingspan of 8 ft., and I learned more about aerodynamics from flying that bird. I and my friend Butch Jones had it win many championships. One day at the meet a

Mr. Shorty Smith flew over in his super cub. He picked a spot close to me to land. It was a bumpy landing. I had never been this close to a real airplane. He got out and introduces himself as manager of the Akron Airport. He was going to be the air marshal of the meet, and was going to hand out awards and trophies to the winners of the events. He told me he left all his trophies back at the airport. He ask if I will like to fly back with him to retrieve them. Would any 16 year old boy have refused this offer? Once we were in the air he had me take the controls He even talked me into a decent landing at Akron, one of the many 1 would make in the future, and that I didn't know about.

He said, "Kid you are a natural". This Monday I would like to see you my office at 8:00 AM sharp! Indeed, I was there at 8:00AM Sharp! Nancy that is how I got into serious flying. And that is what will finance yours and my educational careers and goals.

# The Flying Career Begins

I was excited about a job prospect. Shorty's offer was to help Carl his mechanic to take care of Shorty's fleet. It composed of 2 super cubs.

Cessna 172, a Cessna 182, and a twin engine Beech Travel Air. He used the Travel Air for twin training and the 172 and 182, for commercial rating, then moving up to the travel air for the commercial, multi engine and instrument ratings. All of these licenses were necessary for one to get a job flying for hire. Shorty was tough on being punctual!

My job was to clean and wax the aircraft, keep them gas up, and to make sure the oil level, and tires were inflated to their proper pressure. He also, had Carl mentor me through the A-P course for the mechanics rating. It looks like more than a full time job. He paid me a good salary and my hours began after school from 4:00 to 10:00 PM, 5 days a week. In addition, Shorty would personally give me lessons through the Multiengine, Commercial, and Instrument Ticket.

He figured it would take about 2 years. I should receive all the ratings on my 18th birth day, if I passed all the FAA exam and check rides. Shorty had been an Air Force instructor and I found him to be tough but fair. He kind of filled in for my Dad. Shorty was expecting three war surplus twin engine Beech 18

(C-45), to consummate his contract with the U.S. Postal Service. Shorty had hired 2 Air Force Trained Pilots, Bob, and Jerry. When ready Shorty was going to work me into the fleet. Even though one pilot could fly the cargo version of the Beech 18. Shorty would have me fly as a co-pilot at the age of 17 during my training, for experience. This not out of line, in that the average age of a fighter pilot in WW II ran 19-21years of age. I did most of the flying with Bob or Jerry monitoring me. This gave me all the bad weather flying experience and the different route training into the different airports we were to deliver the high security mail. I knew the time would be short before I became a line pilot and had to do it by myself.

During that period of time I had my pay increase to up to one half pay the line pilots salary, which was $500 a week. It was a super pay for all that I received. I completed my training and was on my own. My first trip was Cleveland, Pittsburg, and Washington.

Boy, you talk about being nervous on takeoff, I had it, but once in the air all the training kicks in. I met Hazel the Desk Clerk and Dispatcher for the first time. I fill out the paper work and before I left for the plane. She said," Have a safe trip and don't "ding" the airplane. Shorty hates that. But she gave a wink of her eye. Something, I found that none of the other guys got. And I did get the flight back without dinging the airplane.

The next morning Shorty gave me my Captains Bars!

But the one thing that followed me through my career, if you want bad weather fly with Don!

(Little did 1 know then I would get to have my skills tested on our return trip back from Washington in a few weeks). To answer your question, Nancy about the new Douglas DC-3's, they will carry about 3x the load of the old Twin Beeches and 50 miles faster, with a longer range. Shorty acquired them from the Monfort Air Force Base in Arizona. They with other World War II Military aircraft are stored in the desert. Southern Air

Line, being a government contractor can have access to the aircraft. Shorty selected two nearly new DC-3's. They are being refurbishing, and painted with our colors of red and white with an aluminum background. Bob, Jerry, and I have been up at Cleveland on the weekends, learning systems and training on the simulators, the DC"3's will be on line in at the end of June. Shorty picked me to be a Captain when we start hiring more crew members, we should all be trained and qualified to fly the DC-3's on line when they come.

To finish our financial picture, since flying for Southern Cargo Air Lines, I average $300-500/week. So our total assets after the wedding will be $35,000, and say if we cash out by next September I should have another $10,000 to our pot of cash. If we stopped work, for whatever reason, we could live comfortably on the interest alone.

I have budgeted out our tuition, books, meals, apartment, rent, so your education to be a teacher is assured. I plan to keep working 4 flights per week. Interesting enough, the Air Force would like this to keep me currant in the DC-3., with upgrading to a business jet.

This will keep me out of the Draft, yet allow me to serve or make a career out of the Air Force, if you and I plan our career path that way. I would advise you to plan on getting your master's in education And a PhD with a master's Degree in Business. I plan on premed and going on to Medical School. That will give us 9 years of formal upper level training and we should have two Doctors in the house.

With that is the is a summary of where I am coming from asset wise, and plan wise. As I said, I have been think about our future a long time and the it over and we talk about it later. 1 would like your input, but now we had better get you home by 5:00 PM as we promised your Mom. You can share your experiences with your Mom tonight, she will understand, maybe. I would like to take your folks to dinner, a place of their choice on March 10. Before going to dinner I would like to ask your parents for your hand in marriage. I hope we don't hit any snags with your parents. I believe Mom is going to be OK with the proposal; however Dad may be a problem. But, I had my two sisters go through this already. Nancy, I will pick you up for Church in the morning.

# The Engagement

I took Nancy to school in our new pickup truck. We went to lunch with her friends. Her best friend mentioned the new pick up, my athletic sweater, and in the change in Nancy's personality. She said, "What is the matter with you'? You act like a different person. And indeed Nancy was, she had a course in maturing. Nancy looked my way and I know what she was thinking: Don if, I told my friends my experiences in this last week they would never believe me, so I won't discuss it further with them and will change the subject. Nancy's thinking had changed well beyond high school. At this point we were thinking past high school and planning our future professions, with only 2 month of high school left.

On a Wednesday the 10th of March was teacher's day. I had been scheduled for the Columbus, Toledo, and Cleveland trip.

Hazel knew our story and made arrangements for me to be back in time for the meeting with Nancy's Parents. I really had confidence in Hazel. I kept her abreast of our situation and trust in her. Shorty had fallen into some bad heath lately, and Hazel was running the show. Later she related to us during this time she felt she had two lives entrusted to her.

I finished my flight with no time to spare and headed to Nancy's house. I didn't have time to change and made sure I had a class "A" uniform on. To my surprise Nancy's Mom and Dad invited us to a "Great Italian Dinner".

Both Nancy and I were somewhat nervous.

After dinner, Nancy's Dad broke the question first: "What is this yon want to marry my last daughter". Young man you really have big plans, how are you going to pay for all of it? With that statement, I took Mr. Kelly aside in another room and gave him a brief of Nancy's and my financial statements and our future plans. He looked me in the eye and his and my eyes met. My eyes that had flown through all the weather and nights, and something must of "clicked". Then he said," How can I refuse".

We all raising glass in a "salute to the new bride".

The last hurdle had been accomplished. It was the first time I kissed Nancy publically gave her Mother a kiss and shook the hand of my new father in law. We set the Date of the Engagement Dinner for both families on 24th of March . As one would have guess it, the place was the "Hartville Kitchen", at 6:00 PM.

I had a scheduled trip: Cleveland, Pittsburg, and Washington, DC. On the 17th of March. I planned to take Nancy with me on this trip.

We had already moved our operations from Akron Municipal Airport to the new Akron Canton Airport.

While in Washington, we could take a taxi across the river to Alexandria, Va. to the "Diamond Mine", where most Washingtonian's go for their jewelry. I will pick you up at 5:00 AM. It will be a long day. We can have a quick bite to eat at the Akron Canton Airport Cafeteria and launch by 6:30 AM.

# "Getting the Rings"

$W$e took off from Akron Canton Airport to collect mail at Cleveland for Pittsburg and Washington, DC. We will have a three hour layover in Washington. Nancy had never been to Pittsburg or Washington, DC. We left Cleveland at 6:30AM for Pittsburg then on to Washington.

I flew a SDF approach down the Potomac River to runway 19 that took us past the White House, Capital Building, and a Washington Monument. We call it the scenic tour in the aviation business. Nancy got to see all of these sites from her cockpit window. She was really impressed! We landed at the Downtown Airport, and were directed to the mail drop area. While plane was being loaded, fueled, and serviced, we took a taxi across the river to Alexandria and the Diamond Mine. "Gus", the gemologist who I previously had him set up in the displaying room , several beautiful bridal sets will be displayed in the $1000 range for Nancy to select.

I am sure she will be pleased with the selection and will find the bridal set beyond her dreams. Gus show us the display room, and Nancy spotted a traditional shaped beautiful bridal set and my matching, rather simple band, all were set in platinum. We gave Gus the sizing of the Mother's rings. The mother's rings: Nancy mother had a large dark blue birth stone surround by diamonds, and my mother a large emerald. Gus suggested we get insurance on all of the rings, which we did. Gus suggested a great little restaurant nearly by we could have lunch while he was preparing the rings. We had a good lunch and were ready to return to the Airport. The rings were prepared and I gave them to Nancy. She had some soft gloves like I suggested to cover up her engagement ring until we were on the plane. She said, "I won't show the ring until it is presented at the engagement dinner". Gus gave us his card, and noted if there is ever a problem to contact him. I told Nancy we need to get your own Uniontown Bank safety deposit box key and make a joint account, we get back home.

# The Trip Back Home from Washington

U pon leaving Washington, the weather report was not good. The cold front that was just east of Chicago was picking up speed and intensity, and coming our way, toward Cleveland, Akron, and Pittsburg. I got clearance to taxi to the active runway 15 at Washington.

In the preflight I obtained ATIS weather briefing, which confirmed the weather forecast. They were, also, predicting heavy snow and icing.

It look like snow storm and prefrontal weather at the Ohio borders and would be reaching the Akron Canton Regional Airport just as it was getting dark. This was a bad combination of events, in that we would get back at the same time. I was filed instruments (IFR) from Washington through Pittsburg to Akron Canton. One of the problems was I had to land at Pittsburg to unload the mail, reload, refuel, before going on. I contacted Washington Control Tower on Frequency 121.7. They gave us clearance to runway 15. Thankfully, we were number two to take off. We were cleared to takeoff and into the overcast at 890 ft.

We contacted clearance delivery on frequency 128.25 that handles all enroute traffic in our sector. Clearance Delivery reminded us of the impending weather conditions. I felt I would brief Nancy when we get to Pittsburg what our options were. Clearance delivery cleared us to 8500 ft. Later Clearance Delivery handed us to Pittsburg Tower for an instrument landing on 28 right. The weather was down to 850 ft. and rather turbulent just before we broke out of the clouds. We taxied to the mail drop area. I ask for expedited service, due to the incoming weather. The ground crew was great and got the job done in record time. I had asked Nancy to go to the bathrooms, but don't linger. When she got back I told her the situation we were in as to the weather and our options. I finished the paperwork and Washington Center clear us to 7500 ft. in route. I figured we had about 15 minutes to spare. I knew we could not make Cleveland. Pittsburg Tower cleared us for taxi and takeoff on runway 23. We entered the clouds at 800 ft. it was turbulent, letting me know the cold front was close. Nancy was very quiet, she probably noted the amount of radio traffic, navigation, and plane operational adjustments do to the rotten weather, which was very rough, and darkness was upon us. If, you had claustrophobia, in a dark cockpit you can't see out, with only instrument lights, is not a safe place to be. Worse than that, you have to depend on your instruments to get you home to safe landing. One had to scan the instrument in "T" scan that took much training in order to not get vertigo, loss of control, and the spiral of death, most aviators are afraid of. Add to this the darkness and turbulent weather and you have a potentially lethal situation. This is what we face that night as we made our way home to Akron Canton Airport. We were in the clouds and snow was pelting our windshield, moderately, however, no serious icing yet. We had deicer boots, but I did want to deploy them yet. About that time Washington Center handed us off to Cleveland Center, and wished us well, I thanked the Controller for his assistance. In a jovially way he said, "We are here to please". Cleveland Center cleared Beech 243 to the Akron Canton Approach on Frequency 125.7.

The Cleveland Controller asked our conditions. I replied," We are in moderate snow, some rime icing, total IRF, and a moderate chop, and we are about 30 minutes from Akron Canton Airport". He asks," What is your alternative airport," I said," Back to Pittsburg." Cleveland Center knew we were a Mail Carrier, and treated us accordingly. Cleveland Center clear's Beech 243 to Akron Canton Approach Frequency 132.05.I contacted Akron Canton's Control Tower. They said, "they were about to close the field to the RVR (runway visual range at minimums)". They cleared us on Runway 23 ILS. It was dark, very turbulent, moderate snow, and in short really rough. I figure I could make one approach before going back to my alternative, I asked approach to turn up the lights on the rabbit (the rabbit is a set of high intensity lead lights to, the runway). Just before we entered the glide slope, and I was setting up my approach speed, props, and gear down, I noticed Nancy seemed to becoming nervous.

I said: "We are almost there, but I have a job for you to do". Check to see the gear is down (two lights), and call it to me, also, look straight ahead look for a line of white lights with a cross on the end. Call this to me when you have it, O.K.?

This made Nancy part of the crew and she forgot her nervousness.

Just about then Nancy called the "gear"", and then the "rabbit'.

I didn't have to tell the tower to turn up the lights on the runway.

They had just made a pass with a snow plow and sweeper up the runway. We barely had enough visibly to turn on to the taxi way and then it was a white out! I called the Tower on 134.75 telling of our plight. The taxi way lights are blue and didn't show up They said," they had visual range a will be a snow plow with a sign on the back flashing follow me. They will get you to the hanger. A that point the tower closed the field. We made it with no time to spare. I called Hazel on the company radio and she said: "I will have 2 cups of coffee for you and Nancy", Carl is getting reading to tow you into the hanger. I can't believe you guys made it in all this weather.

Carl opened the hanger door hooked up the tow to our plane.

He pushed good old Beech 243 into the hanger and put her to bed for the night. Lucky for us all worked as advertised and we had no systems failures, for that is when they always seemed to happen.

When the hanger door closed and we were getting unstrapped, I heard distinct "sighing from the right seat." Nancy that is the second thing I have heard in 2 months; you got to put some oil on it! We both Laughed and deplaned the aircraft. Sure enough in the office stood nervous "mother", Hazel with 2 cups of black coffee. Nancy said: I never drank black coffee before, but she wolfed it down like a naval sailor". I made sure we called the air marshal service to had a guard posted in the hanger to protect the high security mail. If the front passes and the weather clear Bob will take it on the Cleveland in the morning. I got the tire chains out and we made our way to the Hartville Kitchen for supper, after telling Nancy's mother we were having supper there. He mother was worried about getting home due to weather. Little did she know what we just came through, and best she didn't, for I would suggest you don't tell her after we are married.

While eating our dinner, we had a lot of small talk, but Nancy related to me she was really scared in all the weather and was confident in me a professional pilot, I cannot believe you got us through all of that. I said: "With tongue in cheek. It was a walk in the park!"

We got home about 7:00 pm to her nervous mother. I kissed Nancy good night, with the kisses come more frequent and naturally. I gave her mother a kiss and I could tell that please her.

I said, "We have had quite a day". I will pick you up for church in the morning. When we could speak privately. I fold

Nancy put the rings in Safe place and on Monday will get a Key for the safe deposit box at the Uniontown Bank. Rev. Homer's message was great and it spoke to both Nancy and me. I don't think anyone had been through a 24 hr. period we had been through. On the way home from church, we stopped for a light lunch. Nancy said," Is this the way it's going to be? I said: Yes, sometimes". She said:" I don't think my heart will stand it". We both laughed, and I said:" At least it won't be boring". There is an old aviation saying: "Flying is mostly a boring task interlaced with moments of shear terror" Nancy nervously laughed like someone who has been there. Now you know how I make my money. I got her safely home after lunch, gave her a kiss and said:" I will pick you up for school at 7:30 AM." Nancy said:" What a task master you are". I said:" This week will be full, with the engagement dinner meeting with our families ". See you in the morning for school.

# The Dad's Pickup

After Church I went home, my sister Carol had link up with a nice boy she was dating. I talked to Carol, to whom I could trust and ask her to query Dad about his favorite vehicle colors. He had really coveted my truck, but did not want go into debt for one. His old super six Hudson was about to bite the dust, and he wasn't sure how he was going to replace it. It turned out his favor colors were black body with red wheels. I did the same thing with Nancy's and her Dad. She found out her father liked blue. I called Schooners' manager to order both trucks equipped like mine and Nancy's. Luckily they had both trucks in stock. Dad's would be ready on would be ready on Wednesday and Nancy Dad's on Thursday. Nancy's Dad's had a 1938 Plymouth, rusted out, and was in the shape my Dad's was in. He was in no financial shape to finance a wedding. In my long term planning I accounted this in my budget, and getting financial advise from Mr. Smith I was able to get "Fleet Cars Pricing for all the pickups for $3500". (At 1953 Prices).

I told Dad Wednesday late afternoon 1 had to go to Schooner's to check an adjustment on my truck. I drove my truck and he reluctantly took his Hudson, Mom came along. There in the showroom was the pickup of Dad's dreams. Black and shiny with red wheels and trick out like mine and Nancy.

As he was admired the new truck the Manager came over and handed Dad the keys, and said: I want the keys to your Hudson. Dad said: "There must have been a mistake"! No the Pickup was a gift from you son, and is paid in full. Dad was overwhelmed, and he grabbed me and gave me a hug. Do you have a problem with your truck? No, but it was a way of getting you here. I said to the manager perhaps you could give Dad and test drive to get familiar with the truck. By the way Mom, You, Carol, and Dad are invited to Dinner at the Hartville Kitchen at 6:00 PM, Saturday. We have some other surprises then. I would like you to meet Nancy's Parents there, also, for Dinner. They said: "How can we refuse". Ok, we will expect all you at dinner at the Hartville Kitchen at 6:00 PM on Saturday. I used the same "ruse" to capture Nancy's Dad and present him his new blue pickup with a gold strip they were both overwhelmed and grateful. They accepted the Saturday at 6;00PM dinner appointment. I told Nancy it was going to be an interesting night.

# The Engagement Dinner
# at the Hartville Kitchen

The Hartville Kitchen Restaurant is run by the Mennonite Church. It is known for its Home Cooked Meals and Pies. There is several Amish Restaurants in the area and they all have good and fresh food. It will hold 3000 people for dinner. I had asked for a private room for our occasion. I told Nancy not to forget to bring the rings, jokingly. She laughed and said: "How could I after all we went through to get them"? So we gathered together a family for the first time for the engagement dinner. We all gathered at the restaurant at 6:00PM. It was a friendly meeting with everyone introducing themselves.

During the course of the dinner Dad and Nancy's Dad shared identical pickup stories, and for what reasons they became instant friends when it became known they both had a passion for fishing. In fact many of their fishing spots were common to both to them. By to end of the evening they had a fishing date at Mogodore Dam. Mom and Nancy's Mom shared the delivery room for both Nancy and me. I said the grace for the food and the health and success of our family, and settled down to a sumptuous meal. After the meal, we got down to serious business.

I presented Nancy her engagement ring. It looked more spectacular on her finger than before. She put her Mom's Blue/diamond birthstone ring on, she was surprised and in shock at the same time. Then I place Mom's ring on, her birthstone emerald/diamond ring, she had the same reaction. We shared our future plans with the parents. They said:" We did not believe all the things you both had planned to do, but we do now". I believe everyone left dinner that night full of food, and a sense of success as a parent. I felt like we had been released into the adult world. On the way home I asked Nancy, "Did you share with your mother how we got the rings"? Nancy said:" Yes, but I didn't tell her the details about coming back, I don't think her heart would have taken it".

# The Prom Night

After church, following the engagement dinner I said to Nancy, "What about the prom", that started all of this"? She laughed and said: "What Prom"? I said," it will be on the 10th of May with Graduation for the 16th of May". I told her I would like her really look good and to get a nice gown with her mother. Nancy said she had looked at some, but really couldn't afford them. It was good she was looking after our finances, but she said $65.00 would get a nice gown and shoes I said," Plan on it". I plan to rent "tux and shoes", and we will look Spiffy. I am sure there be plenty of school function dances at Kent State she could use the dress. I, also, plan an about $300 for the trousseau for you after the wedding on the Caribbean Honeymoon Cruise. This should help you to stock your wardrobe for college. Nancy looked stunning in her new gown and shoes, and a good time dancing and the banquet before the dance, at the Brookside Country Club. The Prom ended with the playing of "Moonlight Serenade", one of my favorite songs made famous by Glenn Miller. In a way this was the end of our high school days and the beginning of our new life of adventure.

After the prom going home Nancy said? It was being around some teenagers". I laughed and said; "Those kids will stuck in time from the prom". She said, I never thought of it that way.

No one had a plan for the future; they just took what came their way. In fact our high school encouraged and trained people to go into the rubber shops in a job in time they were stuck, became unhappy and unfulfilled, but by that time they had a couple of kids. In a way became trapped by their circumstances. I guess that is why alcoholism and divorce is so prevalent in our community. In my experience with the any jobs I had I saw people on my paper routes like this. I thought I am not going to fit into that cookie mold.

# The Wedding

We decided to have our wedding on June 7th, a Saturday. We will spend the night at the Ritz Calton at Cleveland's Hopkin's Airport, as we planned. The next day we are going to boar d American Airlines Fl. 214 to Ft. Lauderdale FL. There we will board the Holland Line Cruise ship the MS Veendam for a southern cruise of the Caribbean for seven days, then returning home. However, home will be suite 225 in the married section of the Kent State Campus Towers, as we planned and prepared before we left on our Honeymoon, That is the lenitive schedule. We had planned the apartment with one bedroom used an office for study. We will stock it with two large book shelves, two desks, and chairs, a typewriter, paper, pens and pencils, and other things that would make the office functional. The apartment if already furnished with furniture, kitchen table and chairs, living room chairs, lights, and end tables. We can add to this as we need to improve it. Lucky our bed and kitchen linens are included with laundry's service. There is also kitchen utensils and china. Nancy received a lovely set of china as a wedding gift from Southern Airways and will use it for only special occasions.

So all in all we are in good shape. We need to make a shopping trip to the grocery store as a first item when we are back. As of now all of our suppers are taken care of. We need to stock up on breakfast and lunch items. So for the next four years of our life will be busy and I am sure will go fast. I know we were both exciting about the future.

The Wedding was held in the Springfield Fellowship Church, Officiated by the Rev. Homer Burkett. Hazel was there, and was all the pilots, Carl, and of course our family members, and many guests. Nancy had a gorgeous gown. It was a picture perfect Wedding.

The exchange of rings and the final kiss sealing the forever the "Two Soul Mates". The post wedding reception was herded over by our two Mom's. After the reception, we headed to the Ritz Calton Hotel, at Cleveland Hopkin's Airport, and we turned in for the night, excitedly anticipating the cruise tomorrow. Nancy, it seen like we were meant for each other from the beginning. The "Soul Mates" Ring was completed.

# The Honeymoon Cruise

$W$e got board the MS Veendam and had a light dinner then turned in. Both of us were exhausted from the week's events. We awoke on the open seas, a newly married couple waiting for the next adventure to begin. Our first port of call was St. Maarten, an island owned partly by the French and the Dutch. The tale goes that the two countries came to loggerheads of who won the island in a war. To solve the problem, at midway on the island a French man and a Dutch man begin to walk in different Directions and where they met up was the dividing line. It was about equal split of the island. Many of these islands, French, Dutch, and Danish we settled in various ways, such as St, Maarten. Neither Nancy or I had been on a ship this big before, and after showering and dressing we went to breakfast. The ship was Dutch and people on board were from many nationalities. We had meals with a lot of interesting couples. We explored the ship and went to all the shows at night. This was a real experience and when we calculated the shows, meals, extra food any time, and the fact you don't have to move luggage, we found it real bargain In fact we were planning to use this as our vacation in the future.

We visited Antigua, Curacao, Grenada, St. Thomas, and St. Maarten. The Cruise seemed to be over before it started. But all good things must come to an end. We boarded American Airline back to Cleveland after disembarking at Fl. Lauderdale. We got back we retrieved our trusty pickup, threw the luggage into the bed and headed home, in this case are new home at the Kent State Tower Apartments.

I guess when you start out in an exciting life, it seem to continue.

# The Kent State Years

$W$e settled in to our new apartment after the honeymoon. It was all equipped for us and our work prior to the wedding really paid off. We had just a few items to add to make it complete. We made one of the two bedrooms in to an office and the other in to our bedroom. We had a small kitchette and living room.

We had two weeks before the first summer quarter begun. We will need to get registered and take our first classes. The one we decided on was Speech 101. Then in the fall a full load and much work. But we will, by that time, learn the campus and get our fall quarter books, and to find out what professors to have. A distinct advantage over just coming in with one or two weeks to scurry around getting it all together. We register for the Gym, which had just completed a large Olympic sized pool for laps. Nancy did not like to swim and chose another activity. All of this was designed to keep us in shape, especially to keep us alert and also, for my job at Southern Air. During my interview for the Air Force ROTC they noted my professional pilot's status and put me in the accelerated program to be an executive jet pilot flying Saber liners. There were about eight such pilots in my group. Most of them charter pilots. Instead of marching and taking military courses, we were placed in aerodynamics, airframes, engines, etc. Lucky for me they had an advanced training base in my type of airplane at Youngstown Air Force Base, nearby. When I graduated I would have my Air Force Wings and a first lieutenant rank. I also, told the board my intension of going to medical school and entering the Air Force's Aerospace Program. The Air Force Board was delighted with that idea! That would qualify me both a Pilot And a Physician.

This decision was made by Nancy and me as a good career path to follow. That would give us a good retirement at 45-50 years old.

Nancy had courses line up to become a primary teacher and graduate with her license to teach. She talked to her advisor who helps her to a track to take her to a Masters Degree and finally a Ph.D. in Education and a Major in Business. This was what I advised her to do, when she was continent to just get a B.S. in education. She had never heard of this track.

About the 3rd week in June I reported back to Southern Airway or an administrator or both. We were never informed of this training in high school. We were both excited about our college course and the challenges they brought.

About the 3rd week in June I reported back to Southern Airways. Shortly told me both of the DC-3's were finished and on line.

I was to present to America Airline's Training School for a final line check, to be captain on one of them. He asked me:" Who do you want to be your co-pilot"? I said:" Bob". He said:" good choice Don". I will send both of you to Cleveland. On the last week of June just prior to our first quarter at Kent, we were given out new routes. We would fly the southern route on Mon,, Wed., and Friday ( Chicago, Cleveland, Washington D.C., to Cincinnati, Columbus, and Akron Canton). We also, if available, fill in on the Beech,s, to cover for absences.

My salary would be $500 per week. So we were off and running.

I will have to schedule my classes to fit the schedule.

Usually on Sundays we would go to church at the Springfield Fellowship Church, followed by with our parent's dinner after church.

We were normally asked, "How is it going". My response was, worse than a one arm paper hanger! We would laugh and agree. One Sunday I took them out to the flight line to show them our planes. Nancy's Mom saw the twin beech and told Nancy, Don took you to Washington in that, I didn't realize it to be that big?

My Dad said, "You are a captain on the DC-3"? Yes, I am. It is like an Airliner. I showed them the insides of the plane and cockpit Dad said," why did you tell me about this job? Dad I am sure you would not believe it". Later Nancy you can now tell your Mom are trip back from Washington with the rings.

Nancy was assigned to begin her practical teach career from the get go! She was assigned a Kent State Primary Kindergarten Class along with her didactic and theory work. I was told Nancy was a natural. Both of us got "A" in our 1st quarter Speech 101 Course.

My accelerated ROTC program with the saber liner, a twin jet 500+ bullet begun. My instructor said: You won't any trouble flying this bird, this was a great encouragement.

I was able to work out any scheduling problems with Air Force and Southern. I found a professor in the Aeronautics Department who was flying a channel 3 news helicopter in Cleveland, and used it to commute to Kent. We became great friends in the course of four years. With it all being said and done I must say both Nancy and me had a rewarding life in college. Our grade point average for the four years was 3.8 for Nancy and 3.7 for me. I was accepted to Medical School at the University of Nebraska, Omaha. And, somehow, I suspect the Air Force had something to do with it. In 1957, 1 in 40 applicants were accepted. It looks like Nancy would make her goal as a Licensed Primary Grade Teacher. I graduated with a first lieutenant's rank and my wings. And B.S. in Chemical

Engineering. Right next to Omaha is the Strategic Air command Headquarters, better known as SAC. There was a squadron of Saber liners to move the brass around. Almost like airline to Washington, D.C., Andrews Air force Base.

I was told to report to base commander my acceptance to Medical School. The base commander would fast track my reserve orders to Offutt.

I was now on the Air Force's Payroll. It paid $30,000 instead of the $40,000 at Southern. However, all my medical school expenses were paid for, because I will be on the staff. However, we did not have a lot of expenses at KSU and were able to put another $75,000 in our retirement pot. This is going to be a real change for Nancy and me. We had to find a place to live in Omaha, and we started to get the Omaha Herald Newspaper. As painful as it was, I had to tell "Shorty" and Hazel we would be leaving this May. "Shorty" wanted to hold a going away party for Nancy and me.

We sat down with our parents at a Hartville Kitchen Meal and told them of our plans that was somewhat made by the Air Force. They were not happy to see us leave. By then the two rabid fishermen had forge strong bonding between them. They had every lake in northern Ohio even Lake Erie in their fishing sights. So the next Chapter of our life is about to begin.

# The Departure from Southern Airlines

The going away party at the Akron Canton hanger was sad and joyful at the same time. I had been with the airline since its inception. They had me get up and make a speech about its history and the players. Nancy had been on a part time bases for the last four years. I spoke of how Shorty Smith and 1 met and I owned everything to him. Also, Bob, and Jerry for their training of me. I even talked about Hazel how being a "match maker " for Nancy and me, and this turned her face red.

I mention Carl, who kept us flying without incidents all these years. We now have 30 employees, some preparing for the 2 new DC-3's coming aboard to join the fleet. I know Shorty would want me to replace him as he retires in the next two years, but his shoes are too big for me to fill, but Bob can certainly do the job, better than me.

I told everyone about our career paths. Air Force, Medical School, and finally the Air Force Aerospace Programs. We were about to enter. We stated we will never forget you all and fortunate for us to have known you and worked with you, these years.

We hugged and kissed everyone, except Carl. Before we left Nancy went over to Carl embrace him and gave him a large kiss. An thank him for keep me and her safe when we flew. I think

I could see a little moisture in his eyes, for he really like Nancy like a granddaughter and was sad to see her go. Also before we left, they presented Nancy and me two beautiful models of the Southern Airline/ Mail and one of the new DC-3's I was captain in both of them. On the nose was written "Miss Nancy" along with our logo's, red, and aluminum coloring. We then had a toast to the airline and its success. And again one chapter ends in our life and a new and more exciting one begins. However, as a trailer to this chapter, as be got back to the KSU Campus and was finishing the Spring Quarter, and were in preparation to move to Omaha: At one of our briefing at Youngstown AFB, we were advised of the Cuban-Russian Missal crises. This was to get "hot" in a month or so. In fact our base came under "Difficon 5'" meaning the threat of imminent war. When I got back to KSU we went to Southern Airlines. I got our pilots together in secret meeting.

I brief them to get a list of all our airline employees, and make a flight plan to Patagonia (the southern part of Argentina). I told them to be ready to launch out as soon as war was started. I wanted to make sure our families, personnel and their families, and Hazel were aboard. I had an escape plan for Nancy and me. We were all praying this would not happen. As soon as the threat happened it was defused and everyone was relieved

**************

Shorty Smith died in his sleep at age 79, three months later We were all saddened by his passing. To me it was losing my adopted Father. I will always remember him.

# Kent State Graduation and Omaha Transfer

Our graduation from Kent was all that we expected. Nancy got her teachers license, a bachelor of Education Degree, recommendations for graduate school. I got my Bachelor of Chemistry Degree, my Air Force Wings, First Lieutenant Rank, and most importantly my admission to Medical School at Nebraska. Now to find a place to live in Omaha.

We found a nice town house on the "Happy Valley Country Club" not far from the Medical School. It was on the west side of town and relatively close to the University of Nebraska, Omaha. They offered Masters and Ph.D. in Education, at a time Nancy wanted to finish her didactic work. They had build into the program a teachers work program, corresponding to what degree is to obtain. She, also, would have a scholarship stipend, accompanied her appointment.

So for the first time she felt she was going to help earn her way.

The Happy Valley Golf Course apartments we quite spacious compared to our quarters at Kent State. Nancy was really excited about starting school at the University of Nebraska. We even splurged and brought one of the new Motorola Stereos and a bunch of Motovani Records that came out this year.

We can enjoy the stereo for many hours into the future. In fact you can study and keep your concentration even with the soft music playing. Another thing come up: We found we need a second car.

Nancy wanted a silver pick up, and I traded my green truck for another. The price had now risen to $1800 a piece from the original price of $1300. Nancy's school start on the 15th of September and mine on the 25th. so we are all set to go for the new exciting New Year, During my preschool interview we all had to set down before the admission board and tell them what you have done in the past.

After going over my resume there was silence! I thought I am in trouble, and my heart nearly stopped! Dr. Catron the head of Pathology and of this year's board said: "You have lived an incredible life. I want to meet you in my office when we are done with meeting". They knew I was an active pilot on the Saber liner at Offit as an Air Force Reserve Pilot.

My rank had been elevated to Captain. When I met with Dr. Catron, he told me they were trying to service an outstate pathology service. They had a schedule on Monday, Wednesday, and Friday of having a pilot flying a Beech Bonanza to some outstate rural hospitals to gather up frozen sections (a process of doing fast biopsy and calling back the resulted so the surgeon could operate on the same day. Unfortunate early in the fall when the weather turns bad and with no navigation aids the small hospitals and adjoined airstrips. It became hazardous to provide the service. We had a fatal accident due to weather when our plane crashed killing pilot and technician going to their destination. He wanted to know if 1 had any ideas. 1 said:" Yes, I do, you are using wrong equipment to do the job". What do you propose? A Cessna Citation 500 series. Can you fly it? Yes, but I will need a qualified Co-pilot a weather and schedules dispatcher. He or she can work in between flights in the office. The Cessna Citation has short field capability, state of the art color weather radar, and weather forecasting equipment. It is a twin jet 2500 thrust engines and it will fly on one engine.

We have an entering freshman in your class who was an Air Force fighter pilot I will have to meet with him. Dr. Catron said;" We can have lunch together". Jerry turn out to be a perfect fit

With your permission I could have a Citation 500 delivered to Epiley Field in Omaha by tomorrow. Again, Dr. Catron said; "Can you fly it"?

## Jet Cessna Citation 503CC.

Yes, myself and Jerry will have to take the 10 day course of systems and familial training to get typed in the aircraft, because it is over 12,500 pounds. The nest morning we GPS's all the fields that fit the 3000ft/500ft. ceiling criteria, and then we were ready to go!

I can start at 8:00AM and could GPS all of the fields you go into, and have all surgical specimens in the office by noon. Then surgeons then operate and have their patients in recovery by 3:00 PM,

How much will this cost? About $2 to about $3,000,000. He said: I could not do that! You don't have to, lease the airplane, schedule it for all the Universities charter flights, organ transplanting, and advertise any where in the continental U, S,, for meeting, etc. I am sure in a year or two you need another one. We can have the Cessna rep come along and give you the operational costs for fuel, maintenance, and the bottom line will be. I am sure you will be surprised. The Cessna Representative came the next day, and he was really a hit with the Dr. Catron and his staff. They found out it well with in their budget to provide this service.

We found a retired America Airlines dispatcher, tired of retirement, and looking for another job. He was happy to both jobs our dispatcher and the office work in the Pathology Laboratory. Our training went smoothly and Jerry and I were type in the Cessna Citation §00 in no time, plus we worked well together as a team.

The following Sunday we flew all over Nebraska mapping the fields we needed to fly into by noon, then returning to Epply.

Dr. Catron was impressed. We were about 10 days out for starting medical school at this point. We had the schedule set up for Monday, Wednesday, and Saturday to pick up the frozen sections and delivered them to the Pathology Office. They made arrangements with our professors for any tutoring necessary, for any classes we missed. All the lectures were taped. We are now on the medical school's payroll. Within the first week we had an order to bring a "heart organ", the operating Physician and Nurse from Michigan to Omaha. So things were picking up and we were paying our way. I received $35,000 and Jerry $30,000. With extra for organ transfers or special charters, briefed Nancy on all of this and said; I believe we can afford a good vacation she was preparing to write her thesis for the Ph.D.

# The Downfall of Kent State University

Nancy and I noticed a change in culture at KSU. It changed from a friendly place and somewhat of a bedroom community school for all the surrounding communities, to a very liberal school with matching professors coming onboard. It was becoming like Cal Berkley, in California. This seems to lead to an anarchistic culture were anything went. The values we grew with and made us a great nation, paid for in Blood of the Wars past, were cast aside for the unkempt, sloppy clothes, drugs, free sex, disrespect of authority of any kind. The administration loosed all the reins of authority, by saying it was the student's right to act this way. As we all well know it lead to a complete breakdown in all authority, and this led to riots, property destruction, and death. The National Guard were called in to restore order, with the cost of four students losing their lives. It was indeed a sad time with especially the loss of life, reputation, and leadship ship that had to be replaced with those with the fortitude to take charge and get things back in order. This will place KSU in a much needed healing process and warn those who would try to destroy Kent State never to try that again.

It was not hard to go back to the sanity of the University to Nebraska.

We arrived safely in Omaha to start our school year and routine.

At the medical school you have better show up to classes on time with a clean dress shirt and tie.

On the plane home I briefed Nancy about the details of my new job with the university. She was worried about me carrying the load of my responsibility, I said", Not to worry, because we always seem to be one step ahead of disaster".

The Graduation from the University of Nebraska Nancy was awarded her Ph.D. in education and Master in Business. A goal in her wildest dreams she never ever thought of accomplishing. I got my Doctorate of Medicine and up graded to Major, we both graduated in the top of our classes. Bill with his new copilot did a fly over on the graduations ceremony; I figure they lost their job, until I found Dr. Catron was a part of it. He said," His farewell to Nancy and me and wish us well". Hazel kept her promise to retire from Southern. She left when Southern was acquired by FedEx. She felt she was too old to make the move to Omaha, so I thought we could from time to time move the U.S. Air Force to her. She bought a small cottage overlooking Springfield Lake, which made it a clear area for a fly over. So from time to time two F-16 fighter jets would make a low pass over her house. On one such occasion her neighbor said: "What was that? And Hazel would say, "Just a couple of my boys, with a twinkle in her eye", the same one I use to get. It told her we have never have forgotten her. Then one morning she fell asleep in God's Grace. And at her funeral in Springfield four F-16 roared over the cemetery in her honor. The last two went skyward, and If she talk she would of said:, "There goes two of her boys".

Right after graduation my Dad died. In the same year Nancy's Dad died. I guess the two old fishing buddies did not want to fish alone. They got to see Nancy and my success in the accomplishments of our goals. My Mom and Nancy's

Mom attended our graduation exercises from the University of Nebraska, known as the "Big Red".

I was assigned to the Aerospace Medical School Residency, in Dayton, Ohio. I was on the fast tract now, to following my residency of two years to Staff and Command School then War College. All of these things leading to being a Colonel. Nancy was snapped up to head the huge Wright Patterson Airbase's Primary School. It had about 3000 kids in it, and over a one hundred teachers. She was really excited about her new position which was a GS-15 position, the same as mine. So we opened another Chapter in our life.

# The New Kids on the Block

I was to start my residency in Aerospace Medicine on the 15th of September. This left us with most of the summer off. We decided to take a cruise around South America, as had planned in the future. We would start in Fl. Lauderdale, Fl. and go completely around South America. About Peru, Nancy began to have stomach problems.

As we neared Panama. I put in a call for an air evacuation flight to Wright Patterson Air Base. We made it in recorded time. She was put in the hospital of her choice and worked up for her problem. Otherwise I would have taken her to White Hall Medical Center in Texas.

Two Air Force Physicians approached me in the waiting room said," Colonel you are the proud father of two fraternal twins, with the due date in about 5 months". I was flabbergasted to say the least. We would start off with a boy and a girl. Nancy could not believe it!

"Miracles do happen, but not without prayer". Somehow I felt that Hazel had something to do with this whole affair! As soon as the good news was out I had two hovering mother's down from Akron to oversee with the warning you had better call with the first signs of labor!

I knew from this point on that I would have two spoiled Kids with those mothers around. I can hear it now, "Granma does not do it that way". Our Capeheart Housing was excellent. I am sure my rank had something to do with it. The Aerospace Program went well, I passed my Boards and was accepted into War College, which the path to the upper ranks. With the two new kids, our plans changed. I got a nice Fleetwood motorized travel trailer. It we sleep 6 comfortably and we could use it as an overflow quarters for visitor the 2 "Moms", my mom, Nancy's Mom. We all headed back to Akron for a visit and to show off our two new kids. After our visit it was back to work and school. Nancy had taken a maternity leave and it was time to go back however; there was not shortage of baby sitter's. I got my promotion to Colonel and was assigned to the State Department Air Wing.

This put me in contact with pretty important people. The Security Test I underwent was very rigid. In the midst of my assignment Nancy told me was expecting again.

The twins were really growing up fast. I was sure now our choice of professions was the right way.

Time really flew, and the twins were about to enter high school. Jerry and Susan had made their career choices. Time passed quickly! Jerry wanted to go into the Air Force and had applied to the Air Force Academy. Susan wanted to go to the University Nebraska Medical School to become a Family Doctor in northwest Nebraska. And John after college at UNA following his brother footsteps, and both are F-16 Pilots. Susan married the son of the wheat farmer who owns most of the northwest part of Nebraska. They have been fruitful and have three children. Susan still keeps busy part time in the Medical Clinic which has been a godsend to their area. This has been good for her when her children are in school. Our son's now F-16 pilots on their own flew to Akron Canton Airport if anyone knew about the old Southern Air or their father. They ran across "Carl" who was an old retired mechanic who came by for a cup of coffee now and then. As noted FedEx bought out Southern Air. They got to meet "Carl" and spent the morning learning about their father and Mother.

They invited "Carl" to dinner. Guess where? You guess right, the Hartville Country Kitchen. They brought "Carl" up on where their father was doing, and invited Carl down to see Dad and the family. "Carl only had good things to say about their father and mother." On take off they buzzed the field and someone said,"

Who were those guys"? And Carl said," Two of my boys".

We had a shocker at this stage of our lives. My mother died suddenly in January and one week later Nancy's mother died. It was a sad but in a way a joyous time of gathering of all my and family clan to attend two funerals. It was interesting to note both Moms' were wearing the birth stone rings we got them on our engagement. Our youngest son. John's F-16 squadron did the ceremony flight over. We now have become the elder statesmen of our family, before we knew it.

# The Palm Beach Years

After retirement from our jobs Nancy as Dean of University of Maryland's Primary Education Department and myself as Director of the State Department's Air Wing, we had long decided to retire to Palm Beach, Fl. We picked Palm Beach due its ambiance. We selected a Beach side condo overlook the beach and ocean. It was expensive, but we had the income to support it. We had already made arrangements for Jerry, Susan, and John to retire early, if they wanted, but I advised against it. They had begun a family of their own.

Nancy got a large telescope to observe the cruise ships and cargo ships out to sea. She also was learning to use her light signals and the two hoots of their horn really thrilled her. She began to develop the knowledge of the ships and their captains. We had many of days of walking the beach and talking about our experiences together.

They thanked God for all the blessing that he had given them. But now it was time to call us home. In May, in fact the day of the Prom Anniversary they had a good walk on the beach remembering that day so long ago.

They retired to their bedroom for the night.

The next morning they were discovered in eternal sleep in each other arms. The two "soul mates'" had completed their life that God had planned for them and it was time to take them home.

I am sure when they met our savior, Jesus said, "Well done my good and faithful servants"

Matt 19:26

But Jesus beheld them, and said unto them, with men this impossible; but with God all things are possible.

# Post Logue

For those young girls who are waiting for the right person, ask Jesus for his grace and leading, for all he does is never wrong. God makes no mistakes!

# About the Author

## Dr. Ronald W. Hansrote
### BS, MD, FAAFP, FAsMA

Dr. Hansrote is a Biochemistry/Chemistry graduate of Kent State University with post graduate work at Case Western Reserve University's School of Medicine (M.D./PhD Program) in Graduate Physiology and Organic Chemistry. He received his Doctor of Medicine degree from the University of Nebraska and is certified by the National

Board of Medical Examiners. He holds licenses to practice medicine in Nebraska, Florida, and Oklahoma. He is a graduate of the U.S. Naval School of Aerospace Medicine and is designated as a Naval Flight Surgeon/Aviator. He holds the designation of Command Flight Surgeon, USAFR and served on the Shuttle Medical Operations Team for the USAFR's Space Command. He is a Fellow in both the Aerospace Medical Association and the American Academy of Family Practice. He is a fully certified ATP pilot with type ratings for Multiengine Jet Part/135/91 Operations, C-500, Commercial Multiengine and Single Engine Land. Dr. Hansrote is also a certified FAA Advanced Ground Instructor and Senior Medical Examiner. He is the former director of the FAA's Office of Aviation Medicine

(AAM-700) and worked in the Washington D.C. HQ in the fields of Occupational Medicine, Nuclear Medicine, Biological, and Chemical Terrorism and was FAA's Lead Accident Medical Research Officer for the Valu-Jet Fit 592 and TWA Fit 800 accident investigations.

Dr. Hansrote is currently an Associate Professor of Aeronautics at The Florida Institute of Technology. He is married to the former Mitzi Westfall of Akron, Ohio and enjoys deep sea fishing.